# Duck Soup

Jackie Urbanovic

HarperCollinsPublishers

Duck Soup
Copyright © 2008 by Jackie Urbanovic

Printed in the United States of America.

Library of Congress Cataloging-in-Publication Data is available.
ISBN-10: 0-06-121441-8 (trade bdg.) — ISBN-13: 978-0-06-121441-7 (trade bdg.)
ISBN-10: 0-06-121442-6 (lib. bdg.) — ISBN-13: 978-0-06-121442-4 (lib. bdg.)

Typography by Carla Weise
1 2 3 4 5 6 7 8 9 10
❖
First Edition

To Marcia for *everything*, especially the past ten years of generous advice and conversation.

Special acknowledgment to the Marx Brothers for "borrowing" their movie title.

This was it!

A little pepper, some salt, a little parsley and potato—SOUP! This would be Max's masterpiece.

"OOOOOOO-LA-LA!

This is going to be grand."

Max had made lots of soups before—

Fish Soup with Curry
and Pickled Lemon,

Red HOT Chili Soup,
Squash Gumbo,

Cracker Barrel Cheese and
Marshmallow Soup, and Way,
Way Too Many Beans Soup.

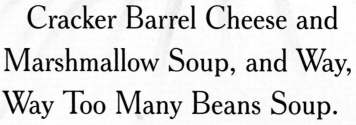

He had cooked them all!
But every recipe had been created
by another chef, not Max.

Now he was making
his own soup.

The soup that *he*, Maxwell Duck,
would be remembered for inventing.

"It needs an herb from the garden! Just wait, my delicate broth. Max will be back to make you *perfetto* in *uno momento*!"

**SMACK!** The front door slammed shut as Brody, Dakota, and Bebe walked in.

SNiFF
SNiFF

"Ooh! What smells so good?" asked Brody.

"Max must be cooking again. I hope it's better than last time!" said Dakota.

# Hey, Max! Maxie!

"Where are yoooooouuuuuu?" called Brody.
"We're about to eat your soup!" added Dakota.

"So—what's wrong?" asked Brody.
"Taste it, already, Dakota!"

Dakota gasped. "I think I know where Max went."

I told him he should never cook alone!

"Call for help!" cried Bebe.

Help!

"There's no time!" said Dakota.

"MAX!
Grab the spoon!"
yelled Dakota.

"That won't work," said Bebe.
"He can't hear you!"

# "I KNOW! THE STRAINER!"

"Strainer?"

"The big bowl with the little holes! GRAB IT!"

Brody hoped that the soup would go down the drain and Max would stay behind.

"AHHHHH!
It's his head!" said Bebe.

"Silly! It's only a potato!"
Brody replied.

# "EYEBALLS!

His eyeballs!" said Bebe.

"Guys, it's only tiny onions!" said Brody.

**"HIS FEET!"** yelled Dakota.

"Calm down, you two! It's only carrot slices!" said Brody.

# SMACK!

They all looked up as the back door slammed shut. Who could that be?

That night Max was very quiet over dinner.

"Cheer up, Max. You're still a great chef," said Irene.

"And you'll cook your perfect soup someday soon," she added.

"And it'll be great!" said Brody.

"Really great!" said Bebe.

"We know you're disappointed," said Irene.
"But at least you're not duck soup."

And they all agreed.

EVEN MAX.